# My Vivid Town

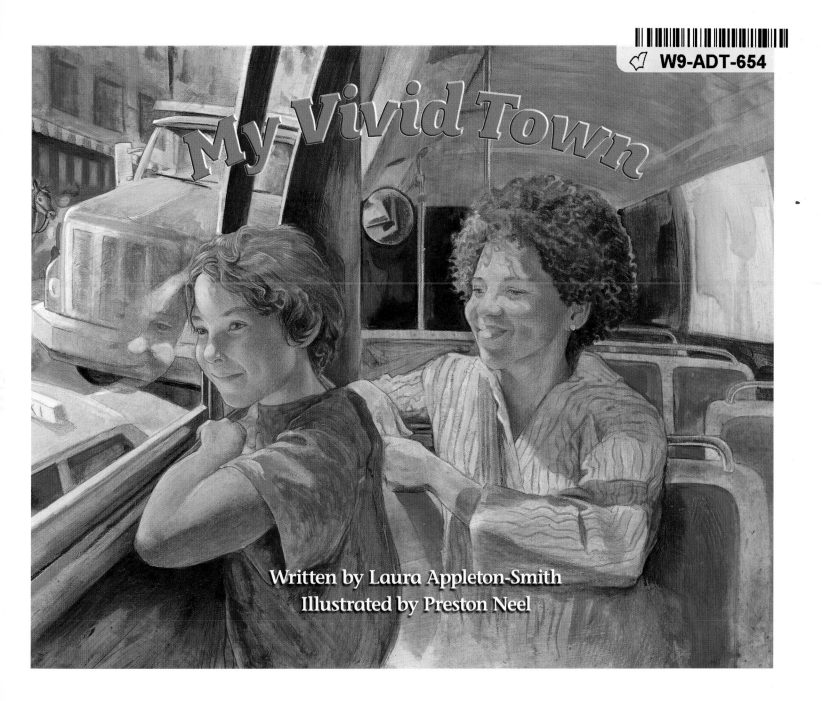

Written by Laura Appleton-Smith
Illustrated by Preston Neel

**Laura Appleton-Smith** holds a degree in English from Middlebury College.
Laura is a primary schoolteacher who has combined her talents in creative writing with
her experience in early childhood education to create *Books to Remember*.
She lives in New Hampshire with her husband, Terry.

**Preston Neel** was born in Macon, Georgia. Greatly inspired by Dr. Seuss, he decided to become an artist at the age of four.
Preston's advanced art studies took place at the Academy of Art College San Francisco. Now Preston pursues his career in
art with the hope of being an inspiration himself, particularly to children who want to explore their endless bounds.

## A Book to Remember™

Published by Flyleaf Publishing
Post Office Box 287, Lyme, NH 03768

For orders or information, contact us at **(800) 449-7006**.
Please visit our website at **www.flyleafpublishing.com**

First Edition
Library of Congress Catalog Card Number: 2007900396
Hard cover ISBN-13: 978-1-929262-61-8
Hard cover ISBN-10: 1-929262-61-2
Soft cover ISBN-13: 978-1-929262-62-5
Soft cover ISBN-10: 1-929262-62-0

*For the devoted reading teachers I have met through my work,*
*and to the many whom I have not met ...*
*Your professionalism and dedication to helping students master*
*the complexities of the English language is invaluable.*
*Thank you for helping to develop a future generation of readers.*

*LAS*

*To Maggie, my beautiful and vivid wife, for all the support and assistance she gives.*

*PN*

At ten o'clock Mom locked our green door
as I skipped down the orange brick steps
in front of our apartment.

I did not step on one black crack
as we went up the block to the bus stop
to pick up the blue crosstown bus.

The white bus door hissed as it locked in back of us.
I dropped our yellow tickets into the glass ticket box.

From the bus I spotted a cop dressed in black.
He was sitting on his big brown horse.

Next to the cop was a big tan dump truck.

Mom and I stepped off of the bus at the market.

Next to the red door was a band with a brass trumpet, a black clarinet, and a set of purple drums.

A dancer in a purple dress clapped her hands
in front of the band.

Her dress had yellow and pink ribbons on the hem.
Her lipstick was red.

Men and women and kids
clapped for the dancer
and dropped dollar bills
into a blue hat
in front of the band.

My Mom lifted a green dollar bill from her pink handbag. She asked me to drop it into the blue hat.

In the market Mom filled a basket with
long orange carrots, big purple eggplants,
a mix of yellow and red peppers,
and six crisp green apples.

We picked up a box of brown eggs
and a glass jug filled with white milk.

Our last stop was to pick up
a pink and red peppermint stick for me
and a brown bag filled with hot nuts for Mom.

We snacked on our peppermint stick and nuts
as we went back to the bus stop
to pick up the blue crosstown bus.

Back in our apartment,
Mom cracked the eggs into a black pan
and added the yellow and red peppers.

Back in our apartment,
Mom cracked the eggs into a black pan
and added the yellow and red peppers.

I sat with a spectrum of colored pens …

And began to color a picture of
my trip to the market in my vivid town.

*My Vivid Town* is decodable with the knowledge of the 26 phonetic alphabet sounds and the ability to blend those sounds together.

**Puzzle Words** are words used in the story that are either irregular or may have sound/spelling correspondences that the reader may not be familiar with.

*Please Note: If all of the words on this page are pre-taught and the reader knows the 26 phonetic alphabet sounds, and has the ability to blend those sounds together, this book is 100% phonetically decodable.*

| Puzzle Words | | "ed" Words | Colors |
|---|---|---|---|
| a | horse | add**ed** | black |
| apartment | I | ask**ed** | blue |
| apples | into | clapp**ed** | brass |
| as | market | crack**ed** | brown |
| began | me | dropp**ed** | green |
| color | o'clock | fill**ed** | orange |
| colored | of | hiss**ed** | pink |
| crosstown | one | lift**ed** | purple |
| dancer | our | lock**ed** | red |
| dollar | she | pick**ed** | tan |
| door | the | skipp**ed** | white |
| down | to | snack**ed** | yellow |
| for | town | spott**ed** | |
| from | was | stepp**ed** | |
| front | we | | |
| her | with | | |
| his | women | | |

## Decodable Vocabulary

| | | | | |
|---|---|---|---|---|
| and | cop | hat | next | spectrum |
| at | crack | hem | not | step |
| back | crisp | hot | nuts | steps |
| bag | cross | in | off | stick |
| band | did | it | on | stop |
| basket | dress | jacket | pan | ten |
| big | drop | jug | pants | ticket |
| bills | drums | kids | pens | tickets |
| block | dump | last | peppermint | truck |
| box | eggplants | lipstick | peppers | trumpet |
| brick | eggs | long | pick | up |
| bus | glass | men | sat | us |
| cap | had | milk | set | vivid |
| carrots | handbag | mix | sitting | went |
| clarinet | hands | Mom | six | |